For my nana, whose memory lives on,
with warm love
DC

In memory of Nana
JC~T

Text copyright © 2020 by Dawn Casey
Illustrations copyright © 2020 by Jessica Courtney~Tickle

All rights reserved. No part of this book may be reproduced, transmitted,
or stored in an information retrieval system in any form or by any means,
graphic, electronic, or mechanical, including photocopying, taping, and
recording, without prior written permission from the publisher.

First US edition 2021
First published by Templar Books, an imprint of Bonnier Books UK, 2020

Library of Congress Catalog Card Number pending
ISBN 978-1-5362-1711-7

20 21 22 23 24 25 TLF 10 9 8 7 6 5 4 3 2 1

Printed in Dongguan, Guangdong, China

This book was typeset in Mrs Eaves.
The illustrations were done in watercolor and digital media.

TEMPLAR BOOKS
an imprint of
Candlewick Press
99 Dover Street
Somerville, Massachusetts 02144

www.candlewick.com

MY NANA'S GARDEN

Dawn Casey

illustrated by Jessica Courtney~Tickle

templar books
an imprint of Candlewick Press

My nana's garden
is tangled with weeds.

"Wildflowers," says Nana,
"food for the bees."

My nana's garden is rainy and wet.

We sing as we gather
with basket and net.

My nana's garden is not very neat.

"Pathways," says Nana, "for very small feet."

In my nana's garden
is a crooked tree.

"A home," says Nana, "snug as can be."

My nana's garden is so dark at night.

There's fire to warm us
and gleams of starlight.

My nana's garden
is full of seeds

with plenty of flowers,
grasses, and weeds.

My nana's garden is lovely and wild.

"Blooming with life,"
Nana says with a smile.

In my nana's garden,
the leaves let go.

On autumn nights the bright stars glow.

My nana's garden is
quiet and bare.

A robin lands
on her empty chair.

In my nana's garden,
I curl up and cry.
The sun doesn't shine
in the winter sky.

My nana's garden lies under the snow.

The world is hushed. Nothing grows.

On windswept branches, new buds swell.

A snowdrop rings its silver bell.

In my nana's garden,
we plant her seeds:
vegetables, fruit,
wildflowers, and weeds.

The seasons turn and our garden grows—

blossoms, berries, peas in rows.

We think of Nana
by the trees.

We sing her song to the bumblebees.

We see her smiling in the flowers

and in the fire of starlit hours.

My nana's garden
is lovely and wild.

"Blooming with life,"
I say with a smile.

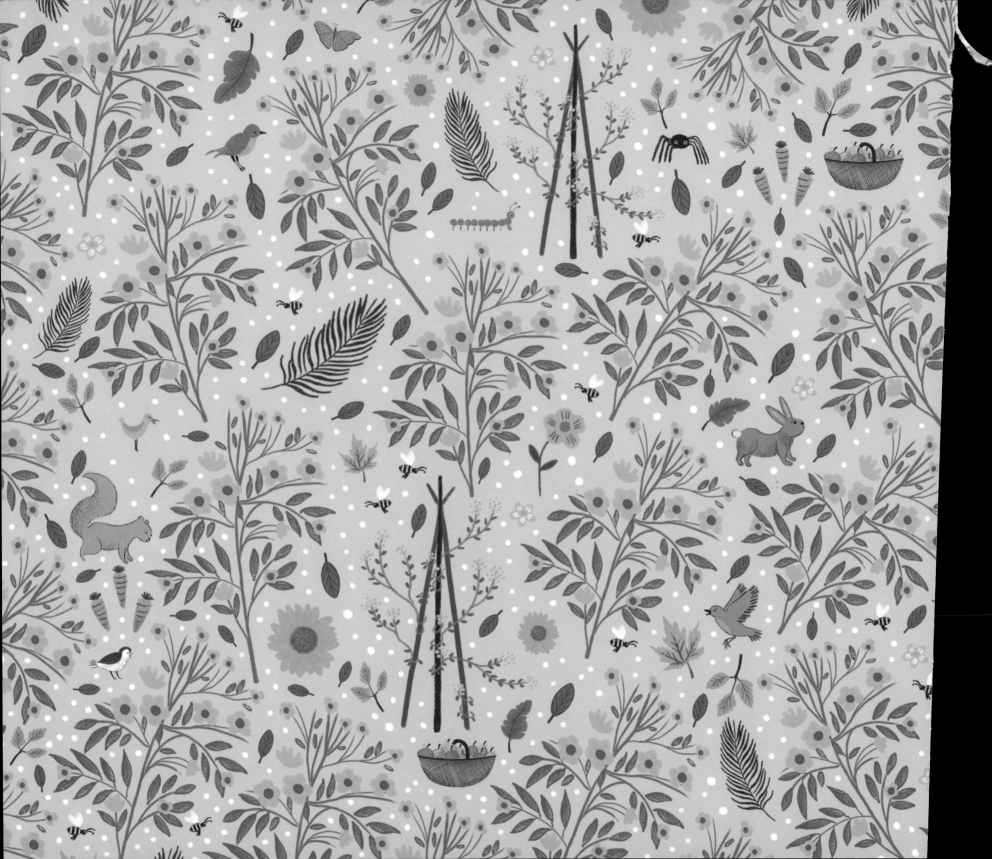